The Summer My Father Was Ten

by ***Pat Brisson***
illustrated by ***Andrea Shine***

BOYDS MILLS PRESS

Published by Caroline House
Boyds Mills Press, Inc.
A Highlights Company
815 Church Street
Honesdale, Pennsylvania 18431
Printed in Mexico.

Publisher Cataloging-in-Publication Data
Brisson, Pat.
The summer my father was ten / by Pat Brisson ; illustrated by Andrea Shine.—1st ed.
[32]p. : col.ill. ; cm.
Summary : A father tells his son the story of how he damaged a neighbor's tomato garden when he was a boy and what he did to make amends.
ISBN 1-56397-435-5
1. Fathers and sons—Fiction—Juvenile literature. 2. Honesty—Fiction—Juvenile literature. [1. Fathers and sons—Fiction. 2. Honesty—Fiction.]
I. Shine, Andrea, ill. II. Title.
[E]—dc21 1998 AC CIP
Library of Congress Catalog Card Number 97-72769

First edition, 1998
Book designed by Jean Krulis
The text of this book is set in 14-point Veljovic Medium.
The illustrations are done in watercolor.

10 9 8 7 6 5 4 3

For Louise Weiss, who understands the importance of stories,
with love and thanks; and in memory of Billy.

—P.B.

In the garden
breath of silver wind
I heard the sea
and was safe.

—A.S.

Every year my father and I plant a garden. Tomatoes, peppers, onions, marigolds, and zinnias grow in neat, straight rows. We pull the weeds that pop up, and we water, mulch, and tend it all through the summer—cutting the flowers to make bouquets for the kitchen table or to give to Mrs. Murowski, our neighbor who broke her hip last winter and has to walk with a cane.

And every spring my father tells me about Mr. Bellavista and the summer my father was ten.

Mr. Bellavista lived alone in the third floor apartment above my father and my grandmother. Plants grew all winter on his windowsill, and in the spring he trudged with rake, garden fork, and trowel to the vacant lot next door to plant a garden. Some years he had to drag away old tires, broken bottles, and other trash before he could even start.

BRIAN BORU
FOR THE BEST FIT
HEAVY WORK BOOTS
PANTS
Yankee Miller

Once his garden was planted, though, you could find him there early every morning—weeding, watering, and watching over his plants. And in the evening he would go and sit on an old wooden folding chair and listen to opera on his radio.

My father didn't know much about the old man, only that he always wore flannel shirts buttoned up to his neck, winter or summer. He didn't talk much to other people who lived in the building, and when he did talk, his accent made his words sound strange. My father and his friends made fun of him sometimes and called him Old Spaghetti Man.

Then one August afternoon when my father was ten, he and his friends were playing baseball near Mr. Bellavista's garden. My father's friend, Nicky, hit a ball over my father's head, and it landed in the middle of the garden. My father ran to get it and found it under a big, leafy tomato plant. The tomatoes were round and red and ripe—just about the size of a baseball. And my father thought, *Boy, I'd like to see Nicky's face if I threw a tomato instead of the ball, and he hit it and it splattered all over him!*

And so, that's what he did—and Nicky *did* hit it and got splattered, just like my father thought he would. My father laughed and laughed, and Nicky chased him back into the garden and grabbed a tomato off the vine and threw it at my father. Then my father threw one at Nicky, and then Joe threw one at Kevin.

Before long, they were all throwing tomatoes and peppers at each other or batting them against the side of the building—the hollow peppers thumping against the bricks and showering thin, white seeds and pulp on the wall and ground, the tomatoes hitting with a *splat* and bursting into messy globs. They even pulled up onions and uprooted the flowers, swinging them around and around over their heads before letting them fly.

They were shouting and laughing so much that they never heard Mr. Bellavista coming. But when Nicky stopped laughing and suddenly stood still, eyes wide and staring, my father turned and saw his neighbor.

He was shaking his head and saying something in Italian. He looked at the walls, splattered with tomatoes and peppers, and at my father and his friends, and he said just one word—"Why?"

My father looked at the garden, trampled and ruined, and it was only then that he realized what they had done. He looked back at Mr. Bellavista, but the old man had gone to his plants and was tenderly picking up the broken pieces and setting them in a pile at his feet.

My father's friends all went away, leaving my father and Mr. Bellavista alone in the lot. My father wanted to go over and tell his neighbor he was sorry, but his feet were like heavy stones holding him there. He watched for a few more minutes and then dragged himself home.

The next morning the mess had been cleared away, the ground raked smooth. There was no way to know that a garden had ever been there. But my father knew.

My father's friends seemed to forget all about what they had done, but my father couldn't forget. Every time he saw Mr. Bellavista, he remembered and wanted to tell him he was sorry, but he just couldn't make the words come out.

Fall and winter came. My father went to school, played with his friends, and almost forgot about what had happened. But when April came again, he remembered.

He watched for signs of his neighbor getting his garden ready, but nothing happened. May came. The sun was warmer, the days brighter, but still Mr. Bellavista made no move to plant.

Finally one day when my father was going up the stairs on his way home from school, he met his neighbor coming down.

"Mr. Bellavista?" my father began. "Are you going to plant a garden this year?"

Mr. Bellavista's eyes looked straight into my father's. "So you can destroy again?" he asked.

"No," my father stammered. "I wouldn't do that. I mean . . . I'm sorry about last year, and I thought maybe I could help."

Mr. Bellavista didn't say anything at first. He studied my father for a few minutes, then rubbed his jaw with the back of his hand.

"Tomorrow," he said at last. "Tomorrow we'll make a garden."

The next day was Saturday. My father and the old man worked all day together. When they were finished, they had a patch of ground carefully raked and planted with tomato and pepper plants, teeny tiny onions, and seeds for marigolds and zinnias. Now when my father looked at the garden, he didn't get a hard knot in his stomach.

Summer came, and every morning my father and Mr. Bellavista checked their plants. My father carried water from his apartment during dry spells and learned to tell what was a weed and what wasn't.

When the flowers bloomed, the old man gave my father bouquets to take to my grandmother. And when the tomatoes were red and ripe (and a little bit bigger than baseballs) and the peppers and onions were ready, my father helped Mr. Bellavista make spaghetti sauce. Then they all ate dinner together in Mr. Bellavista's apartment and listened to opera on the radio.

Every year after that my father helped his neighbor in the garden, until the spring when my father was sixteen and Mr. Bellavista got sick and went to live in a nursing home. Then my father planted the garden himself, and when the flowers bloomed, my father carried bouquets on the bus to his old friend. And when the tomatoes, peppers, and onions were ready, he made spaghetti sauce and put some in the freezer and told Mr. Bellavista that they would have a spaghetti dinner when he came home.

But Mr. Bellavista never did come home.

And now every year my father and I plant a garden—tomatoes, peppers, onions, marigolds, and zinnias in neat, straight rows—and every year I hear the story. . .

. . . of the summer my father was ten.